Michael and the Chicks

by Michèle Dufresne

Pioneer Valley Educational Press, Inc.

One day, the teacher said
to the boys and girls,
"Look! We are going to hatch
some eggs!"

"Wow," said the boys and girls.
"Can we help?"

"Yes," said the teacher.
"You can help
take care of the eggs."

Buon Giorno
Shalom
Hola
Konichiwa
Jambo

Every day, the boys and girls turned the eggs.
"Nothing is happening,"
said Michael.

A week went by.
Every day, Michael looked
at the eggs.
"Nothing is happening!" he said.

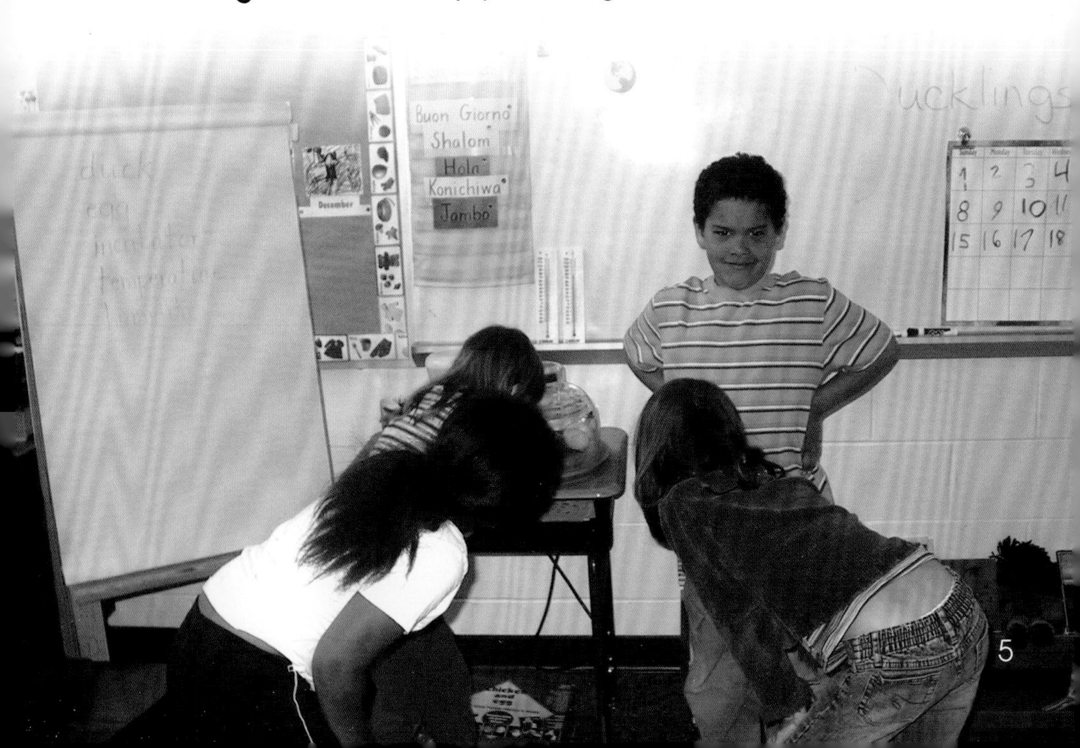

"Let's see if anything
is happening," said the teacher.
"We can look inside the eggs
with this light!"

"Look!" said the kids.
"We can see
the baby chicks!"

One day, there were cracks in the eggs.

"Look!" said Michael.
"The eggs are hatching!"

"Look!" said the boys and girls to the teacher.
"The eggs are hatching!"

THERMOMETER
G.Q.F. MFG. CO
SAVANNAH, GA 31402

Soon there were
seven little chicks.
The boys and girls took care
of the little chicks.

One day, the teacher let
one little chick walk around
the classroom.
Everywhere Michael went
the little chick went, too.

Michael went across the room.
The chick went
across the room, too.
Michael went to the table.
The chick went
to the table, too.

"The chick is following me!" said Michael.

"The chick thinks you're his mother," said the teacher.

"Cluck, cluck," said Michael. "I am a mother hen!"